STAR WARS

HEAD TO HEAD

Pablo Hidalgo

SCHOLASTIC

New York · Toronto · London · Auckland · Sydney · Mexico City · New Delhi · Hong Kong

SCHOLASTIC
www.scholastic.com

Published by Scholastic Inc., 557 Broadway, New York, NY 10012; Scholastic
Canada Ltd., Markham, Ontario; Scholastic Australia Pty. Ltd, Gosford NSW;
Scholastic New Zealand Ltd., Greenmount, Auckland; Scholastic UK, Coventry,
Warwickshire

Scholastic and associated logos are trademarks of Scholastic Inc.

becker&mayer!
BOOK PRODUCERS

Produced by becker&mayer!
11120 NE 33rd Place, Suite 101
Bellevue, WA 98004
www.beckermayer.com

If you have questions or comments about this product, please visit www.beckermayer.com/
customerservice and click on Customer Service Request Form.

Edited by Ben Grossblatt
Designed by Shane Hartley
Design assistance by Richard Anderson, Ryan Hobson, and Tyler Freidenrich
Image research by Zena Chew
Production management by Larry Weiner

Printed, manufactured, and assembled in Jefferson City, Missouri
First printing, January 2010

12 11 10 9 8 7 6 5 4 3 2   10 11 12 13 14 15/0

40

ISBN: 978-0-545-21211-3

10833

INTRODUCTION

Star Wars characters, creatures, and vehicles are pitted against one another in never-before-seen duels! For each matchup, you'll see all the stats and details you need to decide who you think would win . . . and why! The last page features the experts' rulings on each of the battles.

THE DUELS

YODA VS. DARTH VADER

When the Empire came to power, Yoda went into hiding. He never had the right chance to stop Darth Vader. Instead, he waited for decades, until Luke Skywalker was ready to confront his father. But what if circumstances had made it possible for Yoda to face off against the Dark Lord?

YODA

A wise Jedi Master deeply connected to the Force, Yoda does not believe in being a "great warrior." He fights if the Force demands it of him, but aggression is not in his nature.

INFO

Homeworld	Unknown
Affiliation	Jedi
Species	Unknown
Height/Weight	0.66 meters/17 kilograms
Weapons	Lightsaber (green blade)
Special move	Force push

STATS

Intelligence		Strength		Agility	
8	7	4	10	8	4

THE SHOWDOWN

As Yoda approaches 900 years old, he is slowed down not by age but by a spirit broken after the destruction of the Jedi Order. He is not as fast or agile as he once was. Likewise, Darth Vader has had much of his body replaced by machinery. He is slower, and his connection to the Force is not as strong as when he was Anakin Skywalker.

DARTH VADER

Though terrifying, Vader is a bitter, damaged man. He carries in him much anger at being trapped in a mechanical body. This hatred powers him on his journey through the dark side of the Force.

STATS

	8	8	9	8	10	8
Damage		Control		Courage	

INFO

Tatooine	**Homeworld**
Sith, Galactic Empire	**Affiliation**
Human	**Species**
2.02 meters/136 kilograms	**Height/Weight**
Lightsaber (red blade)	**Weapons**
Saber throw	**Special move**

Who wins? See page 64.

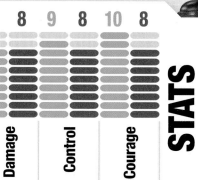

OBI-WAN KENOBI VS. BOBA FETT

Long before he was a hermit, Obi-Wan Kenobi was a Jedi Knight who crossed paths with a ten-year-old Boba Fett, already leery of the Jedi. Fett would grow up to be a notorious bounty hunter. What if these two could somehow meet in their prime?

OBI-WAN KENOBI

A skilled Jedi Knight with quick reflexes and fantastic acrobatic talents, Kenobi nonetheless relies on negotiation whenever possible. He hates piloting, so if he has to fight, he'll do it on the ground.

INFO

Homeworld	Unknown
Affiliation	Jedi
Species	Human
Height/Weight	1.79 meters/81 kilograms
Weapons	Lightsaber (blue blade)
Special move	Spin attack

STATS

Intelligence		Strength		Agility	
8	7	7	8	8	7

THE SHOWDOWN

Kenobi got a taste of Fett hospitality on Kamino, when tangling with Jango. He knows now to eliminate Fett's jetpack as soon as possible. Boba also learned from watching a Jedi kill his father. He'll keep Kenobi at a distance with weapons the Jedi can't parry, like his flamethrower or snare.

BOBA FETT

Boba has had a grudge against the Jedi since the death of his father. He wears a much more battered version of his dad's armored battle suit, and speaks even less than his forebear.

7	7	8	9	10	9

Damage   **Control**   **Courage**

STATS

INFO

Kamino	**Homeworld**
Bounty hunter	**Affiliation**
Human	**Species**
1.83 meters/78 kilograms	**Height/Weight**
EE-3 blaster rifle, heavy carbine, flamethrower, rocket launcher, rocket darts, snare	**Weapons**
Flamethrower attack	**Special move**

Who wins? See page 64.

LUKE SKYWALKER ⓥS. ANAKIN SKYWALKER

An epic duel made impossible by time. The fully grown Jedi Knight Luke Skywalker crosses lightsabers with Anakin Skywalker before his brutal defeat at Mustafar. Both Skywalkers are at the peak of their powers: The Force offers no visions as to the outcome, but neither would emerge unscathed.

LUKE SKYWALKER

No longer an untested youth, Luke is a seasoned Jedi Knight. His hand was cut off in a duel with Darth Vader (and was later replaced with a mechanical hand), and he has learned not to charge impetuously into battle. He fights for a larger purpose: to save his father from the grip of the dark side.

INFO

Homeworld	Tatooine
Affiliation	Rebel Alliance, Jedi
Species	Human
Height/Weight	1.72 meters/77 kilograms
Weapons	Lightsaber (green blade)
Special move	High kick

STATS

7	7	8	9	7	9

Intelligence — Strength — Agility

Both are powerful in the Force and incredibly talented with a lightsaber. Each carries in him the temptation of the dark side. If Anakin gives in, he gains power and lashes out with rage. If Luke rejects its allure, he achieves control and can sidestep and counter Anakin's attacks. The outcome rests in the balance of the Force.

ANAKIN SKYWALKER

Anakin has paid the price for his recklessness with the loss of his lower arm to Count Dooku's blade. This Skywalker also fights for a bigger purpose: to tap into the hidden secrets of the dark side and prevent his loved ones from dying.

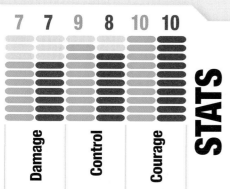

7	7	9	8	10	10

Damage **Control** **Courage**

STATS

Tatooine	**Homeworld**
Jedi, Sith	**Affiliation**
Human	**Species**
1.85 meters /84 kilograms	**Height/Weight**
Lightsaber (blue blade)	**Weapons**
Lunge attack	**Special move**

INFO

Who wins? See page 64.

9

GENERAL GRIEVOUS VS. EMPEROR PALPATINE

During the Clone Wars, General Grievous commanded on the battlefield, but the true power behind the Separatists was the Sith Lord, Palpatine. At war's end, he became Emperor. What if Palpatine had to dispose of Grievous now that the general had served his purpose?

GENERAL GRIEVOUS

Grievous may have a frightening armored exterior, but his rasping cough is a reminder that a soft, living being rests within. Grievous is spry and cunning, adept with both blasters and lightsabers.

INFO

Homeworld	Kalee
Affiliation	Separatist Alliance
Species	Kaleesh Cyborg
Height/Weight	2.16 meters/159 kilograms
Weapons	Captured Jedi lightsabers, electrostaff, DT-57 "Annihilator" blaster pistol
Special move	Four-arm whirlwind with lightsabers

STATS

Intelligence		Strength		Agility	
7.5	10	9	7	9	8

THE SHOWDOWN

Grievous is fast, and with all four lightsabers extended, he becomes a charging windmill of destructive power. To all appearances, Palpatine is a frail and stooped old man. But never forget: He is powered by the full might of the dark side.

EMPEROR PALPATINE

Emperor Palpatine's ambitions have no limits. He has tapped the power of the dark side so deeply that it has made him irrevocably evil. Once, he kept his Sith identity hidden behind a politician's smiles, but now he is evil through and through.

STATS

8	8.5	7	8	5	6
Damage		Control		Courage	

INFO

Naboo	**Homeworld**
Sith, Galactic Empire	**Affiliation**
Human	**Species**
1.78 meters/75 kilograms	**Height/Weight**
Lightsaber (red blade)	**Weapons**
Force lightning	**Special move**

Who wins? See page 64.

Though Senator Amidala will always seek out a peaceful solution, there's just no reasoning with some people. Bounty hunters are a slippery bunch, and shape-shifting hunters are among the most dangerous. But Padmé has experience in deception, so perhaps Zam's disguises won't get past her.

PADMÉ AMIDALA

Padmé is an expert sharpshooter, though she has been trained in more elegant royal blaster pistols rather than heavy weapons. She's not as skilled in hand-to-hand combat as Zam, but she keeps in excellent shape.

INFO

Homeworld	Naboo
Affiliation	Galactic Republic
Species	Human
Height/Weight	1.65 meters/45 kilograms
Weapons	ELG-3A royal pistol
Special move	High kick

STATS

9 5 6	6	6	6
Intelligence		Strength	Agility

THE SHOWDOWN

Zam uses her changeling abilities to surprise her foes, but Padmé's lifetime of security training keeps her on edge. Zam is best equipped for long-range sniping, so she prefers to retreat to a safe distance. Padmé is also a crack shot, having been trained by some of the best bodyguards on Naboo.

ZAM WESELL

Zam is comfortable with rifles, explosives, and poisons. She can change shape to impersonate any humanoid close to her size. She doesn't wear heavy armor because it interferes with her shape-shifting.

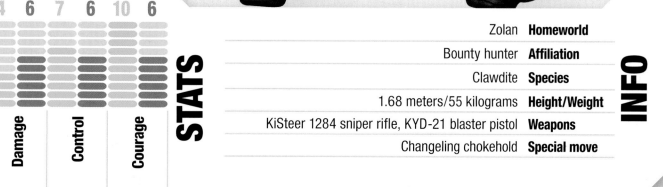

STATS

4	6	7	6	10	6

Damage   **Control**   **Courage**

INFO

Zolan	**Homeworld**
Bounty hunter	**Affiliation**
Clawdite	**Species**
1.68 meters/55 kilograms	**Height/Weight**
KiSteer 1284 sniper rifle, KYD-21 blaster pistol	**Weapons**
Changeling chokehold	**Special move**

Who wins? See page 64.

13

SPEEDER BIKE ⚪ vs. WOOKIEE GNASP

Both are speedy and agile repulsorlift vehicles that can be piloted through the thickest of forests. Neither is built for full-on combat. Instead, they are scout vehicles lightly armed for defense.

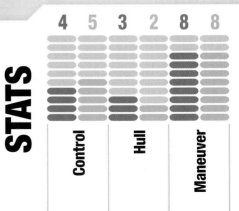

SPEEDER BIKE

The Aratech 74-Z requires only a single pilot. It has a laser cannon slung under its frame. Its forward forks are capped with maneuvering vanes that help in steering.

INFO

Manufacturer	Aratech Repulsor Company
Affiliation	Galactic Empire
Type	74-Z speeder bike
Size	4.4 meters long
Weapons	1 light blaster cannon
Top speed	500 kph

STATS

4	5	3	2	8	8
Control		Hull		Maneuver	

THE SHOWDOWN

Each vehicle is capable of enormous bursts of speed, so the battle arena is likely to be very wide, as the drivers circle each other at tremendous velocity. The first lucky shot will end this match, because each vehicle is thinly armored. Being clipped by a laser bolt would send either one spiraling away to a fiery end.

WOOKIEE GNASP

Also called a fluttercraft, the Gnasp requires a crew of two to operate: a pilot and a gunner. Unlike the speeder bike, the Gnasp gains an advantage by having its weapon face rearward.

STATS

6	6	4	5
Speed		Firepower	

INFO

Appazanna Engineering Works	**Manufacturer**
Wookiee	**Affiliation**
Light fluttercraft	**Type**
7 meters long	**Size**
1 light blaster cannon tail-gun	**Weapons**
310 kph	**Top speed**

Who wins? See page 64.

It's a fierce monster mash as the mighty rancor lumbers out of the pit beneath Jabba's throne room to tangle with the sleek and agile battle-cat often found in Geonosian arenas.

JABBA'S RANCOR

Rancor beasts are found in the untamed jungles of various worlds, though Jabba keeps his confined in an underground pit. The rancor has very tough skin and powerful jaws that can crush bones.

INFO

Homeworld	Dathomir and others
Height/Weight	5 meters/1,650 kilograms
Weapons	Powerful teeth, claws
Special move	Boulder toss

STATS

2	3	15	9	3	10

Intelligence | Strength | Agility

THE SHOWDOWN

The rancor is slow, and trying to grasp the leaping nexu would cause the larger beast much frustration. The nexu's claws and teeth may repeatedly slice the rancor's skin, but all it would take is one solid blow from the rancor to win the fight.

NEXU

A vicious forest feline with keen eyesight, the nexu is a swift climber and jumper. It has razor claws and wicked fangs. Needle-sharp quills stick out from its mane.

9	7	4	9	9	6

Damage **Control** **Courage**

STATS

Cholganna	**Homeworld**
Average 4.15 meters (with tail)/225 kilograms	**Length/Weight**
Sharp teeth, claws	**Weapons**
Tail whip	**Special move**

INFO

Who wins?
See page 64.

The ground will shake when this battle erupts. The massive, crushing wheels of the clone turbo tank push its enormous bulk past any obstacle, while the towering legs of the AT-AT give it the height advantage!

AT-AT WALKER

The gigantic AT-AT has very dense armor, and is armed with two head-mounted laser cannons and a pair of heavier "chin" guns. Its heavy feet also serve as weapons in their own right.

INFO

Manufacturer	Kuat Drive Yards
Affiliation	Galactic Empire
Type	All terrain armored transport
Size	25.5 meters tall
Weapons	2 heavy laser cannons, 2 medium blasters
Top speed	60 kph

STATS

5	4	15	13	1.5	1
Control		Hull			Maneuver

18

THE SHOWDOWN

The tank's bulk is hard to stop once it gets rolling along with its ten huge wheels. It also has no front or back, as it can be driven in either direction—plus, each end is covered with weapons. The AT-AT walker may not be as well armed, but its height will aid its gunner in targeting.

CLONE TURBO TANK

Also known as a juggernaut, the heavy tank is loaded with weaponry: multiple laser cannon turrets, two side-mounted laser cannons, twin blaster cannons, and rocket launchers.

	4	5	10	12
Speed				
Firepower				

STATS / INFO

Kuat Drive Yards	**Manufacturer**
Galactic Republic	**Affiliation**
HAVw A6 Juggernaut heavy armored vehicle	**Type**
49.4 meters long	**Size**
1 heavy laser cannon turret, 2 medium antipersonnel laser cannons, 2 rocket/grenade launchers, 2 twin blaster cannons	**Weapons**
160 kph	**Top speed**

Who wins? See page 64.

If this secret Sith assassin had survived his duel against Jedi Knights Obi-Wan Kenobi and Qui-Gon Jinn, he surely would have relished the chance to battle the mighty Nautolan warrior!

DARTH MAUL

Darth Sidious brutally trained his apprentice to be a weapon of the Sith. Maul is not a schemer like his mentor but a relentless and acrobatic fighter with an extremely dangerous double-ended lightsaber.

INFO

Homeworld	Iridonia
Affiliation	Sith
Species	Zabrak
Height/Weight	1.75 meters / 80 kilograms
Weapons	Double-ended lightsaber (red blade)
Special move	Spin attack

STATS

	6	8	10	8	8	9
	Intelligence		Strength		Agility	

Though both are fast, Maul is more agile. His double lightsaber is slower to swing, but its longer reach can keep Fisto at bay. As a Sith, Maul enhances his attacks with rage. He also uses his imposing appearance to strike fear. Fisto, on the other hand, is one of the most serene and laid-back Jedi in the Order.

KIT FISTO

Kit Fisto is an aquatic Nautolan, with a strong swimmer's build. He has an undeniable spirit of optimism. His thick tentacle-tresses help him remain balanced at all times.

STATS

	6	8.5	8	7	8	10
	Damage		Control		Courage	

INFO

Glee Anselm	**Homeworld**
Jedi	**Affiliation**
Nautolan	**Species**
1.96 meters / 87 kilograms	**Height/Weight**
Lightsaber (green blade)	**Weapons**
Force push	**Special move**

Who wins?
See page 64.

HAN SOLO VS. JANGO FETT

The hotshot smuggler pilot is a quick draw, but is he fast enough to best the bounty hunter who became the foundation of the clone army? What would happen if Han Solo squared off against the father of his greatest enemy?

HAN SOLO

A crack shot and a quick draw with a custom heavy blaster pistol, Solo gets out of scrapes with skill, luck, and the help of a Wookiee companion. He is a talented pilot with a reckless streak.

INFO

Homeworld	Corellia
Affiliation	Smuggler, Rebel Alliance
Species	Human
Height/Weight	1.8 meters/80 kilograms
Weapons	Modified BlasTech DL-44 heavy blaster pistol
Special move	Reckless charge

STATS

Intelligence		Strength		Agility	
6	6	7	7	6	8

THE SHOWDOWN

A fair fight would be a very close contest, so Fett would do everything he could to keep that from happening. He's got an arsenal of dirty and deadly tricks up his sleeves, and he would use every one of them to strike Solo from a distance. Fett's jetpack keeps him far enough out of Han's reach to avoid a lot of damage.

JANGO FETT

The deadliest bounty hunter of his time, Fett wears a high-tech Mandalorian armor suit covered with weapons, including a built-in flamethrower, missile launcher, snare, and jetpack. It ultimately took the great Jedi Master Mace Windu to eliminate Jango.

STATS

6	10	8	8	10	9
Damage		Control		Courage	

INFO

Concord Dawn	**Homeworld**
Bounty hunter	**Affiliation**
Human	**Species**
1.83 meters/79 kilograms	**Height/Weight**
Twin WESTAR-34 blaster pistols, rocket launcher, flamethrower, snare, rocket darts, climbing blades	**Weapons**
Flamethrower attack	**Special move**

Who wins? See page 64.

JEDI STARFIGHTER VS. TIE INTERCEPTOR

It's a tangle of small, lightweight, speedy attack craft—and it's sure to be a battle that's far too fast to track with the naked eye.

JEDI STARFIGHTER

The tiny Delta-7 Jedi fighter is extremely compact and carries two laser cannons. It has an onboard astromech droid to handle emergency repairs.

INFO

Manufacturer	Kuat Systems Engineering
Affiliation	Jedi
Type	Delta-7 Aethersprite-class interceptor
Size	8 meters long
Weapons	2 dual laser cannons
Top speed	1,260 kph (in atmosphere)

STATS

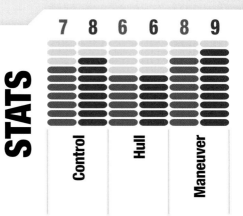

7	8	6	6	8	9
Control		Hull		Maneuver	

24

THE SHOWDOWN

Both fighters boast the most advanced ion engines of their time, pouring all their energy into velocity. Only light shields protect the Jedi fighter, while none at all envelop the TIE craft. It's up to each pilot's skill and the fighter's twisting maneuvers to keep from being blasted into cinders.

TIE INTERCEPTOR

The fastest of the standard TIE models, the interceptor sports four laser cannons, one on each wingtip. Its daggerlike wings are covered with solar panels to add power to the ship.

8	10	5	6
Speed		Firepower	

STATS

Sienar Fleet Systems	**Manufacturer**
Galactic Empire	**Affiliation**
Twin ion engine interceptor	**Type**
9.6 meters long	**Size**
4 laser cannons	**Weapons**
1,250 kph (in atmosphere)	**Top speed**

INFO

JAWA VS. EWOK

The planets Tatooine and Endor occupy almost opposite points in the galaxy, but what if a native of each world had reason to fight—say, over a certain golden droid? Don't let their short stature deceive you: A wise Jedi once said, "Size matters not!"

JAWA

A Jawa can tolerate extreme heat. It's a smelly scavenger, but is highly resistant to disease. Jawas are skittish, only traveling in groups and within the safety of their massive sandcrawlers—but are excellent at ambushing their prey.

INFO

Homeworld	Tatooine
Affiliation	None
Height/Weight	Average 0.97 meter/30 kilograms
Weapons	Ionization blaster
Special Power	Nasty stench

STATS

5	5	4	6	7	4
Intelligence		Strength		Agility	

Much would depend on where the battle took place, as each alien would have an advantage in its native environment. A Jawa may have more high-tech devices, but those devices are designed to take out droids, not living beings. The Ewok is stronger, more brawny and stout, while the Jawa is scrawny under his robes.

EWOK

A spiritual being of the forest, an Ewok is fiercely loyal and protective of its groves and family. It carries primitive wood and stone weapons, yet is surprisingly strong. Ewoks are known as terrible pilots, but seem to have luck on their side.

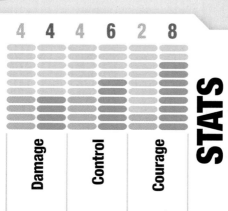

STATS

4	4	4	6	2	8
Damage		Control		Courage	

INFO

Forest moon of Endor	**Homeworld**
Rebel Alliance	**Affiliation**
Average 1.2 meter/50 kilograms	**Height/Weight**
Spear, stone axe, bow and arrow, sling	**Weapons**
Vine swing-attack	**Special Power**

Who wins? See page 64.

It's a clash of interstellar titans as these immense warships exchange broadsides of heavy turbolaser fire. A Trade Federation battleship may be imposing, but how does it stack up against the might of the Imperial Navy's flagship?

STAR DESTROYER

The Empire's proud warship is dotted with turbolaser and ion cannon emplacements, which are designed to take out other warships. Beyond that, its holds are filled with TIE fighters and other combat craft.

INFO

Manufacturer	Kuat Drive Yards
Affiliation	Galactic Empire
Type	Imperial-class Star Destroyer
Size	1,600 meters long
Weapons	60 turbolaser cannon and 60 heavy ion cannon emplacements, 10 tractor beam projectors
Top speed	975 kph (in atmosphere)

STATS

Control		Hull		Maneuver	
7	6	160	200	1	1

The ring-shaped Trade Federation battleship is larger than the triangular destroyer, but it is an outdated craft built at a time when the galaxy was at peace. The Star Destroyer has a much better arrangement of weapons, while the battleship has many gaps in its defenses. Each, however, sports massive cannons capable of inflicting much damage.

TRADE FEDERATION BATTLESHIP

These battleships began life as freighters fitted with weaponry to guard the goods within. Not designed to be warships, they have weaknesses that can be exploited, especially by small ships.

4	3	25	15

Speed **Firepower**

STATS

Hoersch-Kessel Drive, Inc.	**Manufacturer**
Trade Federation, Separatist Alliance	**Affiliation**
Lucrehulk-class combat freighter	**Type**
3,170 meters long	**Size**
42 quad laser emplacements	**Weapons**
500 kph (in atmosphere)	**Top speed**

INFO

Who wins?
See page 64.

Clone troopers, the fighting forces of the Galactic Republic, paved the way for the rise of the Empire. The armies of Imperial soldiers no longer have the Jedi Knights to command them—or get in their way. Unlike clone troopers, though, not all stormtroopers are created equal.

CLONE TROOPER

Clone troopers are created from Jango Fett, the galaxy's most skilled bounty hunter. They are physically identical, highly trained, and greatly superior to battle droids. They follow orders to the letter.

INFO

Homeworld	Kamino
Affiliation	Galactic Republic
Species	Human clone
Height/Weight	Average 1.83 meters/80 kilograms
Weapons	DC-15S blaster rifle, DC-15A blaster rifle
Special move	Martial arts

STATS

Intelligence		Strength		Agility	
5	5	7	6	5	5

THE SHOWDOWN

Clone trooper training emphasizes squad operations, but compared to stormtrooper training, much more time is spent on individual survival. Clone troopers are therefore better at improvising. During the Empire era, the Jango Fett clones were joined by other clone sources, leading to stormtroopers of uneven quality.

STORMTROOPER

After Jango's death, the lack of fresh genetic material meant the Empire added clones from other sources as well as nonclone soldiers into the ranks, eventually creating the modern stormtroopers. Not the best of shots, they can be effective at times—even deadly.

STATS

6	6	7	5	8	8
Damage		Control		Courage	

INFO

Various	**Homeworld**
Galactic Empire	**Affiliation**
Various	**Species**
Average 1.83 meters/80 kilograms	**Height/Weight**
E-11 blaster rifle, DLT-19 heavy blaster rifle	**Weapons**
Targeted strike	**Special move**

Who wins? See page 64.

31

BANTHA VS. REEK

Not dangerous under most circumstances, banthas and reeks are still wild animals and, as such, can be unpredictable. Banthas are smarter than reeks and are easily domesticated. This means they can be trained to attack on command, whereas a reek will most likely strike if startled or threatened.

BANTHA

Banthas tend to be docile, but when alarmed they can become a trampling menace. Their horns are strong, but not as sharp as a reek's.

INFO

Homeworld	Tatooine and elsewhere
Height/Weight	Average 2.5 meters (at shoulder)/1,000 kilograms
Weapons	Horns
Special move	Trample

STATS

4	2	14	15	2	5

Intelligence   Strength   Agility

THE SHOWDOWN

In this fight, the contestants would literally butt heads. Neither the reek nor the bantha builds a strategy around surprise attacks; each would announce its charge with a lot of snorting and stomping. The repeated thunderclap of horns colliding would wear each animal down, turning this fight into a grueling endurance contest.

REEK

Reeks are not ordinarily dangerous, but the ones used for fighting are often abused and starved until they are highly aggressive. Their massive horns and tough skin make them very formidable.

STATS

7	9	4	5	5	5

Damage **Control** **Courage**

INFO

Codian Moon	**Homeworld**
Average 2.24 meters/1,100 kilograms	**Height/Weight**
Teeth, horns	**Weapons**
Bite	**Special move**

Who wins?
See page 64.

MILLENNIUM FALCON VS. SITH INFILTRATOR

The fastest hunk of junk in the galaxy versus one of the stealthiest cutting-edge ships the galaxy has ever seen. Can the patchwork freighter survive a confrontation with Darth Maul's high-tech pursuit craft?

MILLENNIUM FALCON

The *Falcon* is very fast, and its shields and weapon power are downright illegal. It has two turret-mounted quad laser cannons and carries concussion missiles.

INFO		
Manufacturer	Corellian Engineering Corporation
Affiliation	Smuggler, Rebel Alliance
Type	Modified YT-1300 light freighter
Size	34.75 meters long
Weapons	2 quad laser cannons, 2 concussion missile tubes, 1 antipersonnel blaster
Top speed	1,050 kph (in atmosphere)

STATS

Control			Hull		Maneuver
5	5	5	6	7	7

THE SHOWDOWN

The Sith Infiltrator carries a cloaking device. It remains invisible to sensors until Maul is ready to strike. Though this is a considerable advantage, the *Millennium Falcon* is well armed and armored. Its greatest enemy, perhaps, is itself, as its repeated modifications result in wildly uneven operation and unpredictable malfunctions.

SITH INFILTRATOR

Darth Maul's ship, dubbed the *Scimitar*, may not be as powerful as the *Falcon*, but it is hard to hit, thanks to advanced sensor baffling technology that causes it to disappear from targeting screens.

STATS

7	8	6	7
Speed		Firepower	

INFO

Republic Sienar Systems	**Manufacturer**
Sith	**Affiliation**
Infiltrator star courier	**Type**
26.5 meters long	**Size**
6 concealed laser cannons	**Weapons**
1,180 kph (in atmosphere)	**Top speed**

Who wins? See page 64.

R2-D2 VS. IG-88

The resourceful astromech droid known as R2-D2 is not built for combat, but he will do just about anything to save the day. IG-88 is a soulless engine of destruction that will stop at nothing to annihilate its preprogrammed target.

R2-D2

Loaded with hidden gadgets and tools, R2-D2 is usually underestimated by bigger droids. His booster rockets and oil sprayer can work together to create a fiery surprise. Above all, R2-D2 shows bravery well beyond his programming.

INFO

Homeworld	Naboo
Affiliation	Rebel Alliance
Manufacturer	Industrial Automaton
Droid type	Astromech droid
Height/Weight	1.1 meters/32 kilograms
Weapons	Electroshock prod, circular saw, arc welder
Special move	Shock

STATS

Intelligence		Strength		Agility	
5.5	5	4	8	4	7

THE SHOWDOWN

IG-88 is typically equipped with a wide variety of powerful blaster rifles, explosives, and edged weapons. While R2-D2 may outsmart IG-88, avoiding incoming fire with a clever smoke screen, all it will take is one good shot to overload the astromech's circuits.

IG-88

IG-88 pays no attention to how much destruction it causes when targeting a victim. An assassin droid with no master, it is one of the most dangerous droids in the galaxy.

STATS

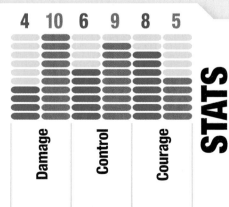

4	10	6	9	8	5
Damage		Control		Courage	

INFO

Holowan Laboratories	**Homeworld**
Bounty hunter	**Affiliation**
Holowan Mechanicals	**Manufacturer**
Assassin droid	**Droid type**
1.96 meters/140 kilograms	**Height/Weight**
Pulse cannon, riot gun, sonic stunner, thermal detonators	**Weapons**
Sonic blast	**Special move**

Who wins? See page 64.

TIE FIGHTER VS. NABOO N-1 STARFIGHTER

One vessel is a work of art, handcrafted in an era of pride in workmanship. The other is an assembly-line combat craft churned out in the thousands by the factories of the Empire. How do these signature vessels that define their respective eras compare?

TIE FIGHTER

Its twin ion engines give the TIE its name and its stunning speed. The huge hexagonal wings are solar panels that give extra energy to the ship's systems.

INFO

Manufacturer	Sienar Fleet Systems
Affiliation	Galactic Empire
Type	Twin ion engine space superiority fighter
Size	6.3 meters long
Weapons	2 laser cannons
Top speed	1,200 kph (in atmosphere)

STATS

	5	5	5	6	7	7
	Control		Hull		Maneuver	

THE SHOWDOWN

TIE Fighters are designed for swarm attacks. A TIE pilot is at a disadvantage in one-on-one dogfights; although TIE Fighters are fast, they are fragile. They do not have shields. The Naboo fighter is shielded, but its hull is comparatively weak. Both carry twin laser cannons.

NABOO N-1 STARFIGHTER

The Naboo fighter carries twin proton torpedo launchers, but the speedy TIE would likely outmaneuver them. An N-1 can more easily take a glancing hit due to its shields.

7	8	6	7
Speed		Firepower	

STATS

Theed Palace Space Vessel Engineering Corps	**Manufacturer**
Naboo	**Affiliation**
Royal starfighter	**Type**
11 meters long	**Size**
2 laser cannons, 2 proton torpedo launchers	**Weapons**
1,100 kph (in atmosphere)	**Top speed**

INFO

Who wins?
See page 64.

JABBA THE HUTT VS. JAR JAR BINKS

Neither contender is the fittest specimen of his species, but frighteningly obese versus dumb luck could prove interesting. Jabba is used to having his henchmen do his physical tasks for him. Though Jar Jar comes from a proud warrior culture, he's a clumsy misfit.

JABBA THE HUTT

An old Hutt, Jabba has extremely dense and tough skin. He is slow, but his massive bulk makes it difficult to get a grip on him or subdue him. He can also slobber impressively.

INFO

Homeworld	Nal Hutta
Affiliation	Criminal
Species	Hutt
Height/Weight	1.75 meters/1,358 kilograms
Weapons	None
Special move	Crushing roll

STATS

Intelligence		Strength		Agility	
6	6	8	5	1	4

THE SHOWDOWN

Jabba could be dangerous, *if* he were to raise his rear from his reclining platform. With a snap of his tail and a roll of his massive bulk, Jabba could stun and squash his foe. But fortune often smiles on Jar Jar. He has bumbled into dangerous situations before, and stumbled out of them with barely a scratch—while his defeated foes have been left scattered across the field.

JAR JAR BINKS

At times an awkward outcast, Jar Jar is agile, but often zigs when he intends to zag, which confuses opponents who think the Gungan is cleverer than he really is. His heart is in the right place, but he is easily frightened into risky acts.

STATS

5	4	2	3	5	5
Damage		Control		Courage	

INFO

Naboo	**Homeworld**
Galactic Republic	**Affiliation**
Gungan	**Species**
1.96 meters/66 kilograms	**Height/Weight**
Gungan boomer	**Weapons**
Tongue lash	**Special move**

Who wins? See page 64.

Some say the Rebel Alliance X-wing won the war against the Empire, but what if it had been flown a generation earlier, during the time of the Clone Wars?

X-WING

The Incom T-65 X-wing lacks overwhelming strengths and weaknesses, unlike other specialized ships. Its wings carry four laser cannons, and its hull has two proton torpedo launchers. An astromech droid assists with in-flight repairs.

INFO

Manufacturer	Incom Corporation
Affiliation	Rebel Alliance
Type	T-65 space superiority fighter
Size	12.5 meters long
Weapons	4 laser cannons, 2 proton torpedo launchers
Top speed	1,050 kph (in atmosphere)

STATS

Control		Hull		Maneuver	
6	5	8	11	7	5

THE SHOWDOWN

The X-wing pilot would lock the ship's wings in attack position, giving its laser cannons greater accuracy. The Rebel fighter packs a bigger punch, but any pilot would have difficulty damaging Grievous's ship with its stronger armor. It would also reply with devastating proton torpedoes, though it's not as agile as the Rebel craft.

GRIEVOUS'S STARFIGHTER

The *Soulless One* is customized to General Grievous's tastes. It has triple blaster cannons as well as a sophisticated sensor jamming system. It is coated in very strong Impervium armor.

	Speed	Firepower	
7	7	8	6

STATS

Feethan Ottraw Scalable Assemblies	**Manufacturer**
Separatist Alliance	**Affiliation**
Belbullab-22 starfighter	**Type**
6.71 meters long	**Size**
2 triple laser cannons	**Weapons**
1,100 kph (in atmosphere)	**Top speed**

INFO

Who wins? See page 64.

ACKLAY VS. BOGA

A flurry of teeth and spikes, an angry acklay combines the worst parts of an insect and a dinosaur. If this terrifying monster were to threaten Obi-Wan Kenobi, Boga wouldn't run from danger. She's a brave varactyl that would gladly charge into battle.

ACKLAY

Found in dangerous jungles, the acklay can tear into prey with its spikelike arms. Its armored frill protects its neck. It has poor eyesight, but compensates by lashing out with a long reach.

INFO

Homeworld	Vendaxa and elsewhere
Height/Weight	Average 3.05 meters/1,200 kilograms
Weapons	Sharp teeth, stabbing claws
Special move	Shaking bite

STATS

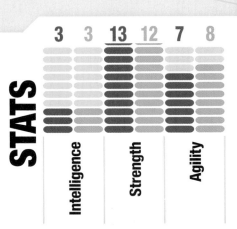

3	3	13	12	7	8
Intelligence		Strength		Agility	

THE SHOWDOWN

Boga doesn't come with as many dangerous appendages as the biting, stabbing acklay. She's tough and fast, however, able to run circles around the beast. Boga's tail could lash out at her enemy's legs. If knocked off balance, the acklay would have trouble righting itself and might be down for the count.

BOGA

Intelligent, loyal, and brave, Boga is a swift runner. Her feet can climb along very steep surfaces, and her beak is both strong and sharp. She uses her long tail mainly for balance, but can employ it as a weapon.

STATS

9 5 5 7 6 8

Damage

Control

Courage

INFO

Utapau	**Homeworld**
Varactyl	**Species**
15 meters/1,150 kilograms	**Length/Weight**
Beak, spiked tail	**Weapons**
Tail swipe	**Special move**

Who wins? See page 64.

ARC-170 VS. B-WING

Each is among the most heavily armed starfighters of its generation. These combat fliers are designed to take on targets much larger than themselves. Now their multiple weapons are pointed at each other!

ARC-170

The ARC-170 fighter is designed to fly solo and mount a solid defense. Aside from its medium wing-mounted laser cannons, it has two rear-facing laser cannons and carries six proton torpedoes.

INFO

Manufacturer	Incom/Subpro Corporation
Affiliation	Galactic Republic
Type	Aggressive Reconnaissance Starfighter
Size	14.46 meters
Weapons	2 aft blasters, 2 medium laser cannons, 6 proton torpedoes
Top speed	1,050 kph (in atmosphere)

STATS

Control		Hull		Maneuver	
7	6	7	8	6	5

The B-wing's wingtips are capped with heavy ion cannons that can disrupt all power in the ARC-170 . . . *if* they connect. The ARC-170 is much more maneuverable than the big, lumbering targets the B-wing usually battles. If the B-wing tails the ARC, its pilot had better look out for the ARC's tailgunner!

B-WING

A bizarre ship designed by an alien mind, the B-wing carries three heavy ion cannons, a heavy laser cannon, twin cockpit-mounted blasters, and a pair of proton torpedo launchers.

STATS

6	Speed
6	
8	
10	Firepower

INFO

Slayn & Korpil	**Manufacturer**
Rebel Alliance	**Affiliation**
Heavy attack starfighter	**Type**
16.9 meters tall, 4.7 meters long	**Size**
2 proton torpedo launchers (8 torpedoes), 3 ion cannons, 2 auto blasters	**Weapons**
950 kph (in atmosphere)	**Top speed**

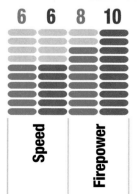

Who wins? See page 64.

CHEWBACCA VS. WAMPA

The wampa's savage howls can drown out the winds of Hoth! Chewbacca's growls rattle the trees of Kashyyyk! Two fur-covered titans lock muscled arms to determine which is the fittest: a Wookiee warrior from the forests, or a wampa from the frozen plains.

CHEWBACCA

Chewbacca is fiercely strong, known to pull his enemy's arms from their sockets. A gifted mechanic, Chewie keeps the cranky *Millennium Falcon* running. His preferred weapon is a bowcaster, or laser crossbow.

INFO

Homeworld	Kashyyyk
Affiliation	Smuggler, Rebel Alliance
Species	Wookiee
Height/Weight	2.28 meters/112 kilograms
Weapons	Bowcaster
Special move	Arm-ripper pull

STATS

Intelligence		Strength		Agility	
6	3	10	12	4.5	3

THE SHOWDOWN

Cover your ears as both wampa and Wookiee bellow in rage. Assuming Chewbacca has somehow lost his bowcaster weapon, he must fight the wampa hand-to-clawed-hand. The wampa may be stronger, but Chewie is faster and smarter than the furious beast. If Chewie's friends are in danger, he will never surrender!

WAMPA

The deadliest hunters from a frozen planet, wampas are surprisingly stealthy for their size. Their enormous paws are capped with sharp claws. Their strength can subdue even an adult tauntaun.

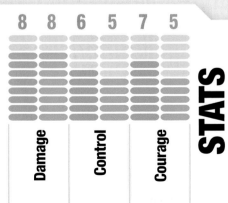

STATS

8	8	6	5	7	5
Damage		Control		Courage	

INFO

Hoth	**Homeworld**
Average 3 meters/150 kilograms	**Height/Weight**
Claws, fangs, horns	**Weapons**
Face swat	**Special move**

Who wins? See page 64.

49

PRINCESS LEIA VS. AURRA SING

Princess Leia has been trained in self-defense and has spent all her adult life targeted by the Empire. Aurra Sing is a deadly assassin, capable of challenging even Jedi Knights. What if the Empire hired Sing to do its dirty work?

PRINCESS LEIA

Even though she spent much time in the public spotlight, Leia has a secret sensitivity to the Force. She is a great shot with a blaster and is a fearless and inspiring leader.

INFO

Homeworld	Alderaan
Affiliation	Rebel Alliance
Species	Human
Height/Weight	1.5 meters/49 kilograms
Weapons	Drearian Defender sporting blaster
Special move	Fast draw

STATS

9	6	6	6.5	5	7
Intelligence		Strength			Agility

The heartless Aurra Sing is eager to face new adversaries, and Leia is a hard target to find alone or defenseless. If Sing couldn't connect with her rifle or twin blasters, she'd relish fighting at close range, so she could look her opponent in the eye. Princess Leia is every bit as brave.

AURRA SING

Aurra was raised and trained by assassins. The solitary Sing doesn't rely on technology as much as other hunters do. If unarmed, she can use her long, sharp fingers to cut and tear skin.

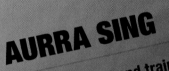

4	6	7.5	7	10	6
Damage		Control		Courage	

STATS

Nar Shaddaa	**Homeworld**
Bounty hunter	**Affiliation**
Human hybrid	**Species**
1.74 meters/56 kilograms	**Height/Weight**
Czerka Adventurer sniper rifle, paired blaster pistols	**Weapons**
Clawed swipe	**Special move**

INFO

Who wins? See page 64.

BOSSK VS. DROIDEKA

With bloodshot eyes, scaled skin, and sharp teeth, Bossk is a ruthless bounty hunter. He has even been known to eat his opponents! But he's not likely to find a shielded and armored destroyer droid very appetizing.

BOSSK

As a reptilian Trandoshan, Bossk is hardy to the extreme. He can even grow back lost limbs, though doing so takes time. He is skilled in heavy weapons and explosives, but has a nasty temper that sometimes gets the best of him.

INFO	
Homeworld	Trandosha
Affiliation	Bounty hunter
Species	Trandoshan
Height/Weight	1.9 meters/113 kilograms
Weapons	Blaster rifle, grenade launcher
Special move	Raking claws

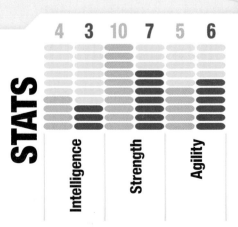

STATS

4	3	10	7	5	6
Intelligence		Strength			Agility

THE SHOWDOWN

After softening up the droideka with thermal detonators and grenades, Bossk would shift to his blaster rifle. If the destroyer droid wanted to move about, it would have to drop its shields, at which point Bossk would blast away until he'd shredded it. The droideka, for its part, would return fire with its laser cannon arms—and Bossk has no shield.

DROIDEKA

Droidekas fold up into wheel shapes and roll into combat. When unfurled, they project a blaster-proof deflector shield, but destroyer droids must deactivate it to move about on their pointed legs. Their arms are powerful blaster cannons.

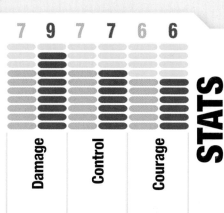

STATS

7	9	7	7	6	6
Damage		Control		Courage	

INFO

Colla IV	**Homeworld**
Trade Federation, Separatist Alliance	**Affiliation**
Colicoid Creation Nest	**Manufacturer**
Destroyer droid	**Droid type**
1.83 meters/75 kilograms	**Height/Weight**
Two sets of twin laser cannons	**Weapons**
Tumble charge	**Special move**

Who wins? See page 64.

SNOWSPEEDER ⚪ VS. ⚪ ATTACK GUNSHIP

Among the most heavily armed and armored aerial repulsorcraft are the flying combat vessels of the Rebel Alliance and the Galactic Republic. Both provide essential air support for their ground soldiers, but now they're pitted against each other in a dogfight to the finish!

SNOWSPEEDER

Formerly an Incom T-47, this airspeeder has been equipped by the Rebel Alliance with combat armor and beefed-up weapons. Its two cannons face forward, while its harpoon and tow cable face to the rear.

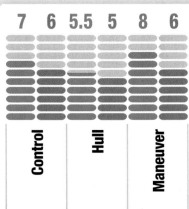

INFO

Manufacturer	Incom Corporation
Affiliation	Rebel Alliance
Type	T-47 modified combat speeder
Size	5.3 meters
Weapons	2 laser cannons, 1 power harpoon and tow cable
Top speed	1,100 kph

STATS

		Control		Hull		Maneuver
7	6	5.5	5	8	6

As a ground support craft, the gunship is slower and less maneuverable than the Rebel snowspeeder. It does, however, pack much more weaponry, some of it capable of damaging the speeder at long range before it gets close. The speeder's tow cable could make things interesting.

ATTACK GUNSHIP

A larger vehicle designed to ferry troops to the battlefield, the gunship bristles with weapons: two rocket launchers, four wing missiles, four laser turrets, two chin turrets, and one rear cannon.

7 6 5 10

Speed

Firepower

STATS

INFO

Rothana Heavy Engineering	**Manufacturer**
Galactic Republic	**Affiliation**
Low-altitude assault transport/infantry (LAAT/i) gunship	**Type**
17.4 meters long	**Size**
3 antipersonnel laser turrets, 2 missile launchers, 4 laser turrets, 8 light air-to-air rockets	**Weapons**
620 kph	**Top speed**

Who wins?
See page 64.

LANDO CALRISSIAN VS. GAMORREAN GUARD

A real duel of opposites: Lando Calrissian, with his intelligence and charm, against one of Jabba's lumbering, yet dangerous guards. Lando found himself face-to-face with one of the tuskers while undercover in Jabba's palace, but the time wasn't right for causing trouble.

LANDO CALRISSIAN

Cardplayer and rascal, Lando hates combat but has had his share of experience. He'd much prefer a clever bluff, a crafty con, or a business deal than a fight.

INFO	
Homeworld	Unknown
Affiliation	Rebel Alliance
Species	Human
Height/Weight	1.78 meters/79 kilograms
Weapons	Hold-out blaster
Special move	Bluff

STATS

	8	4	6	8	5	3
	Intelligence		Strength		Agility	

THE SHOWDOWN

Lando wouldn't be able to smile his way out of trouble with *this* opponent, so he would turn to his tiny, concealed blaster for protection. The Gamorrean guard, known for his warlike ways, would respond how he always does: with brute force.

GAMORREAN GUARD

On their homeworld, Gamorreans live in clans headed by powerful sows and warlord boars. A Gamorrean, working for Jabba or not, prefers hand-to-hand combat.

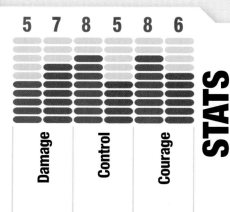

STATS	
Damage	5 7 8
Control	5 8
Courage	6

INFO	
Gamorr	**Homeworld**
Criminal	**Affiliation**
Gamorrean	**Species**
Average 1.8 meters/100 kilograms	**Height/Weight**
Arg'garok war axe	**Weapons**
Axe chop	**Special move**

Who wins? See page 64.

Y-WING VS. VULTURE DROID

One of the oldest vessels in the Rebel Alliance arsenal, the Y-wing was flown on missions during the Clone Wars. In that time, it undoubtedly was harried by the seemingly endless starfighters of the Separatist droid army.

Y-WING

Not as fast or flashy as an X-wing fighter, the outdated Y-wing is still a tough, reliable attack bomber. It carries a turret-mounted ion cannon, twin laser cannons, and proton torpedoes.

INFO

Manufacturer	Koensayr
Affiliation	Rebel Alliance
Type	BTL-S3 attack fighter
Size	16 meters long
Weapons	2 laser cannons, 2 light ion cannons, 2 proton torpedo launchers
Top speed	1,000 kph (in atmosphere)

STATS

Control		Hull		Maneuver	
5	7	8	4	5	7

58

THE SHOWDOWN

The Y-wing is a glutton for punishment, able to absorb a lot of damage before it flies apart. A vulture droid isn't terribly powerful, but could win the contest with a well-fired homing missile. A Y-wing pilot can defend the ship's rear quarters, as long as the crew includes a tailgunner to operate the ion cannons.

VULTURE DROID

Speedy and insectoid, these chatty battle droids can transform from ground-walker mode to a sleek fighter-craft. Not very creative, they fight best in groups. They are fragile, but agile.

STATS

6	7	9	6

Speed — Firepower

INFO

Xi Char Cathedral Factories	**Manufacturer**
Trade Federation, Separatist Alliance	**Affiliation**
Droid starfighter	**Type**
3.5 meters long	**Size**
4 blaster cannons, 2 energy torpedo launchers, can also carry a buzz droid launcher	**Weapons**
1,180 kph (in atmosphere)	**Top speed**

Who wins? See page 64.

MAGNAGUARD DROID (VS.) ROYAL GUARD

Each of these warriors is tasked with the fearless protection of their masters. For the MagnaGuards, it is their programming that compels them to charge into battle to defend General Grievous. Loyalty to Emperor Palpatine runs deep into the Royal Guards' very souls.

MAGNAGUARD DROID

These IG-100 droids are trained in multiple forms of unarmed combat. Out of his entire droid army, General Grievous is most pleased with his MagnaGuard soldiers.

INFO

Homeworld	Various
Affiliation	Separatist Alliance
Manufacturer	Holowan Mechanicals
Droid type	IG-100 series bodyguard droid
Height/Weight	1.95 meters/123 kilograms
Weapons	Electrostaff, DT-57 Annihilator blaster pistol
Special move	Staff twirl

STATS

Intelligence		Strength		Agility	
5	7	9	9	6	6.5

60

A staff for a weapon is more ceremonial than practical, yet each warrior can use it extremely well. The swift Royal Guard leaps about like a red ghost, and the MagnaGuard is equally nimble. Through discipline, a Royal Guard can ignore most pain. A droid, on the other hand, doesn't feel it at all.

ROYAL GUARD

Royal Guards undergo vigorous physical training at a secret facility, learning exotic martial art forms such as echani. They are drawn from the best stormtroopers in the Empire.

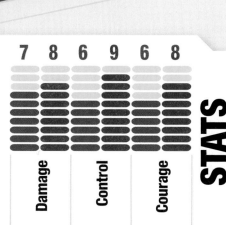

STATS

7	8	6	9	6	8
Damage		Control		Courage	

INFO

Various	**Homeworld**
Galactic Empire	**Affiliation**
Various	**Species**
Average 1.8 meters/80 kilograms	**Height/Weight**
SoroSuub Controller FP force pike, heavy blaster pistol	**Weapons**
Pike stab	**Special move**

Who wins? See page 64.

GUNGAN VS. TUSKEN RAIDER

Both cultures have had an uneasy relationship with human colonists. Tusken Raiders are primitive and will savagely attack intruders on their lands. Gungans, too, prefer to be left alone, though in time they came to work alongside humans on Naboo. Still, the territorial instinct runs deep in both species.

GUNGAN

Members of a proud warrior culture, Gungans produce brave soldiers called militiagungs. Their unusual technology includes electrically charged spears and plasma globes called boomas, which the Gungans hurl with great accuracy.

INFO

Homeworld	Naboo
Species	Gungan
Height/Weight	Average 1.9 meters/75 kilograms
Weapons	Cesta and atlatl to hurl boomers, electropole
Special move	Booma blast

STATS

Intelligence		Strength		Agility	
7	5	7	8	6	4

THE SHOWDOWN

Considering each species' native environment, "home field advantage" would make a big difference. Gungans get dried out by the hot desert air, and Sand People would find the swamps of Naboo intolerable. Both are skilled with clubs. At long range, Gungans use spears while Tuskens have sniper rifles, but limited ammunition.

TUSKEN RAIDER

Sand People will fiercely protect their territory. They carry a traditional club-axe called a gaderffii, or gaffi, stick. They can be easily startled, but will regroup and return in greater force.

STATS

7	6	6	6	8	6
Damage		Control		Courage	

INFO

Tatooine	**Homeworld**
Tusken	**Species**
Average 1.9 meters/89 kilograms	**Height/Weight**
Gaderffii (gaffi) stick, sniper rifle	**Weapons**
Gaderffii gash	**Special move**

Who wins? See page 64.

THE EXPERTS' PICKS